Quentin Blake

MISTER MAGNOLIA

RED FOX

OTHER BOOKS BY QUENTIN BLAKE

Mrs Armitage on Wheels
Mrs Armitage and the Big Wave
Mrs Armitage Queen of the Road
Nursery Rhyme Book
Fantastic Daisy Artichoke
The Green Ship
All Join In
Clown
Cockatoos
Simpkin
Zagazoo
Loveykins
A Sailing Boat in the Sky
Quentin Blake's ABC

MISTER MAGNOLIA
A RED FOX BOOK

First published in Great Britain by Jonathan Cape,
an imprint of Random House Children's Books

Jonathan Cape edition published 1980
Red Fox edition published 1999

1 3 5 7 9 10 8 6 4 2

Red Fox Books are published by Random House Children's Books,
61–63 Uxbridge Road, London W5 5SA,
a division of The Random House Group Ltd,
in Australia by Random House Australia (Pty) Ltd,
20 Alfred Street, Milsons Point, Sydney, NSW 2061, Australia,
in New Zealand by Random House New Zealand Ltd,
18 Poland Road, Glenfield, Auckland 10, New Zealand,
and in South Africa by Random House (Pty) Ltd,
Endulini, 5A Jubilee Road, Parktown 2193, South Africa

THE RANDOM HOUSE GROUP Limited Reg. No. 954009
www.kidsatrandomhouse.co.uk/quentinblake

A CIP catalogue record for this book is available from the British Library.

Printed in China

Mr Magnolia has only one boot.

He has an old trumpet

that goes rooty-toot —

And two lovely sisters

who play on the flute —

But Mr Magnolia has only one boot.

In his pond live a frog

and a toad and a newt —

He has green parakeets

who pick holes in his suit —

And some very fat owls
who are learning to hoot —
But Mr Magnolia
has only one boot.

He gives rides to his friends
when he goes for a scoot —

And the splash is immense
when he comes down
the chute —

But Mr Magnolia

has only one boot.

Just look at the way that
he juggles with fruit!

The mice all march past
as he takes the salute!

And his dinosaur!

What a MAGNIFICENT

brute!

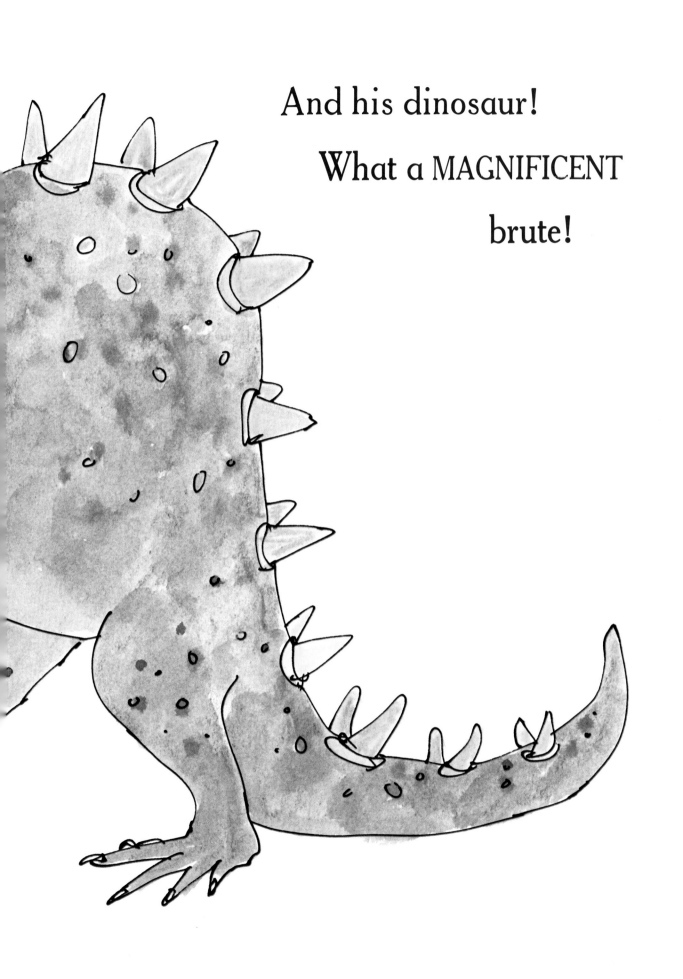

But Mr Magnolia —
poor Mr Magnolia!
— Mr Magnolia
has
only one boot . . .

Hey —

Wait a minute . . .

Now then . . .

Keep going . . .

What's this?

Look!

It's a boot!

It's a boot!

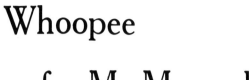

Whoopee
for Mr Magnolia's
new boot!

Good night.

I know what
to call him!

What shall we call Wibbly's Puppy?

Mick Inkpen

Hodder Children's Books

A division of Hachette Children's Books

Wibbly Pig has
a new puppy.
'Aaaaah, isn't he lovely!
What shall we call him?'
'He's not very big,'
says Tiny Pig.
'We should
call him. . .

WITHDRAWN

Other Wibbly Pig books:

Everyone Hide from Wibbly Pig
In Wibbly's Garden
Is it bedtime Wibbly Pig?
Tickly Christmas Wibbly Pig!
Wibbly Pig's Silly Big Bear
Don't Lose Pigley, Wibbly Pig!
Wibbly Pig likes bananas
Wibbly Pig likes dancing
Wibbly Pig likes to have fun
Wibbly Pig likes pictures
Wibbly Pig likes presents
Wibbly Pig likes playing

Tiny!
Just like me!'

'It would be much
funnier if we called
him Big!' says Big Pig.
'No, it wouldn't!'
says Tiny Pig.
'Yes, it would!'
'No, it wouldn't!'

It is just as
well that the
Pig Twins have
arrived.

No, it wouldn't!

I still
think
Tiny
is a
good
name.

'We should call him **Patch!**' say the Pig Twins, pointing to the patches on their heads.

The Twins agree that Patch is an excellent name.

But nobody else does.

Everyone thinks and
thinks and thinks and thinks.
But the more they think,
the more nothing happens
inside their heads.

'Let's find Pig Ears
and ask him,' says
Wibbly Pig. 'He's good
at thinking.'

What's
wrong with
Tiny?

Pig Ears thinks
for a very long time.

He thinks for so long the puppy wanders off

and does a little poo.

Then
he falls
asleep.

At last Pig Ears speaks. . . .

'He's got nice sticky up ears,' says Pig Ears. 'Why not call him Ears?'

It is the worst suggestion yet.

Spotty Pig arrives. But before he can say anything, everyone says, 'We're not going to call him

Spot!

(Besides, it's been done before.)

So what are we going to call him?

Can't anyone think of a good name?'

Along comes
Scruffy Pig.
'I like your
new puppy!'
says Scruffy Pig.

We all stare at
Scruffy Pig.
We all stare at
the new puppy.
'Look at them!
Look!

They're **identical!**'

I don't know
what 'identical'
means!

'It means he's exactly the same!' says Scruffy Pig. 'Exactly the same as me!

And my name is **Scruffy,** so we should call him **Scruffy,** too!'

'Scruffy Two!'
says Wibbly Pig.
'That's what we'll call him!

It's
even
better
than
Tiny!

It's better than Tiny!
It's better than Big!
It's better than
Patch, or Ears,
or Spot.
It's perfect!'
says Wibbly Pig. . .

'Woof!'
says Scruffy Two.